THIS Won't WILL HURT

THE NEXT TEN YEARS

CARA DEE

This Won't Hurt

The Next Ten Years

Copyright © 2023 by Cara Dee
All rights reserved

Edited by Silently Correcting Your Grammar, LLC.
Formatted by Eliza Rae Services.

AN EXTENDED EPILOGUE of THIS WILL HURT II

For when the characters can't say goodbye.
(And the author can't say goodbye to them either.)

CHAPTER 1
2020

We got married!
July 14th, 2020
Monroe Samuel Finlay & Jacob Casper Denver

...tied the knot on this fantastic day up in Big Sur. Please enjoy this masterfully edited video of our ceremony, attended by Haley Denver, Seth Diaz, Russell and Nikki Astor, and our children. At the end, you'll find an invitation to one hell of a wedding reception that doesn't have a date or venue yet. Stay tuned for the end of the pandemic!
Much love,
Roe and Jake

Roe Finlay

"Pleeeease! You see how I'm *begging*, Mom?" Colin peered imploringly into the laptop screen. "Cas! Come beg with me! We might crack them!"

I chuckled and stayed in the patio doorway.

Jake sat on the couch in the living room next to Colin, arms folded over his chest, reluctance written all over him.

And, of course, Cas came running out of their room and joined Jake and Colin on the couch.

"Please, please, please, please," Casper pleaded. "And you know we have the best idea in the whole world!"

I sighed and scrubbed a hand over my mouth, and I exchanged a glance with Jake. We were understandably on the fence; Colin wasn't even ten yet, and at this rate, Casper might start first grade in a couple weeks on a freaking computer. We'd crossed all our fingers for the damn pandemic to end, but it seemed unlikely this year. Everything was shut down.

Nikki coughed on her end. She and Russell were on their second week of being sick with Covid. "Jake, gimme your thoughts again."

Jake shrugged and scratched an eyebrow. "They can still count their ages on both hands, and they can't take something like this back. Once it's out, it's out. Doesn't matter if it's 'just a YouTube series.' They'll be exposed to all our followers."

"Until we get our own channel," Colin added smugly.

Slow your roll, buddy. We haven't agreed yet.

Yet.

I suppressed another sigh, wavering a whole lot. It wasn't as if the boys were gonna do anything that might embarrass them in the future. It was a nature documentary for children, shot in our own backyard. But even so...they were incredibly young, and the internet wasn't always a friendly place. If we eventually agreed, we would have to protect them from all the interactions. Plus, Colin came out strong but tended to fade quickly when it came to being in the spotlight. He could be just as introverted as Jake.

"It's only ten episodies." Casper flashed seven fingers. I wavered some more. My boy still thought it was fun to say episodies, for chrissakes. "It's little."

"And short!" Colin chimed in with. "Like, maybe twenty minutes long."

Nikki chuckled through a cough. "Boys, can you excuse Dad and me for a moment? And get the good-cop daddy?"

I laughed. "I'm right here."

"Why am I the bad cop?" Jake frowned.

As the boys scurried back to their room, I sat down next to Jake.

"How you doin', hon?" I asked.

"Eh. Getting better, but it still sucks," she replied hoarsely. "You can stop sending us Panera delivery, though. We have a fridge full of soup now."

I grinned.

"I'm waitin' for my answer here," Jake pointed out. "Am I the bad cop?"

"No, you're not." I put my hand on his knee. "Thing is, if it weren't for this damn lockdown, I would've stood firm way longer. But the boys are running out of things to do."

The other three were easier to entertain. Between our backyard and the pool at the Condor Chicks house, they were having a great summer. We were teaching Sam how to swim, and the two youngest goofballs couldn't get enough of being in the water.

3

"It would be a nice project for them," Nikki agreed. "Jake, honey, I think it might be time to let them do this. They wanna take after you guys. It's sweet."

Jake furrowed his brow. "I don't have any problem whatso-ever with them running around with their cameras. Hell, I'm proud. It's the whole taking things public that concerns me."

Valid point; couldn't stress that enough. But I had to mention something to Nikki, because I was so impressed by Colin's mind. "We actually told them we could go camping and do a documentary just for us, and Colin was like, but we wanna do this in the backyard because lots of kids can't go anywhere during lockdown, and we can show them there's wildlife at home."

"Aww." Nikki went into the "I'm melting" momma mode and looked to Jake. "Let them do the damn docuseries, Jake. I have all the faith that you and Roe will edit it into something they'll look back on one day with pride."

Jake was caving. He missed editing too. Right now, there wasn't much we could do. We did have work waiting—and a larger project in the researching stage, though that was mostly my job. I was reading a fuckload this year, which, of course, had triggered our work brains. Everyone today was looking to books, TV, and movies to make the days go by faster. Seth had barged into the office one day and just exclaimed, "Push content! Push content, push content, push content!"

We needed content.

Our numbers were ridiculously high on our podcast and whatever we put on YouTube.

"Can we compromise?" Jake proposed. "Five episodes, fifteen minutes long, and we'll see how it goes. It'll take about a day to put together one episode, editing included—okay, maybe two days—so we can continue on short notice if we don't run into trouble."

"Absolutely," Nikki coughed. "What does Haley think?"

"She's on board," I replied. "She suggested we could dedicate one day of the week to the boys on our Insta. None of us is ready to consider them having their own channels and accounts—"

"Definitely not," Jake agreed.

"But if that day comes, Haley will find someone to manage it," I finished. "Bottom line, the boys are too young to be exposed to social media interactions. Hell, Haley filters our shit too."

"That sounds great," Nikki said. "I can't wait to see what you come up with! Our babies are growing up."

"A little too fast," Jake muttered.

Nikki logged off shortly after, and the living room became silent.

The boys would probably run back out soon to hear the verdict.

Jake leaned back against the cushions with a heavy sigh, and he pulled me with him. With my head on his shoulder, I glanced at him and waited him out. He didn't look too troubled anymore. In fact, the corners of his mouth twisted up a bit, and he tilted his face at me.

"So this is it," he murmured. "Our story ends, and the boys are the new stars."

I rumbled a laugh. He could be funny sometimes. He might be the one who cared the least about stardom in LA.

His eyes flashed with amusement.

I reached up and kissed him. "The boys might become stars, but our story will never end."

He smiled and kissed me back. "I like the sound of that."

On August 4th, we started filming *Little Species with Casper Finlay and Colin Denver* in our backyard. The boys were fucking cute. Jake filmed, and I could tell he'd committed to the project. He was a proud father, looking through the viewfinder as Colin introduced beetles and butterflies to future fans.

My job had been to help the boys put together a concept. I had researched the species, printed out illustrations, and rehearsed trivia and quick facts with primarily Colin. Casper was, much like his dad, the comic relief. He had no interest in parroting lines, but he was a natural sidekick who provided good questions and funny responses.

I watched the boys in the front yard here and there; Colin was currently talking excitedly about a butterfly sitting on a flower, while...while Cas was rolling around in the grass in the background. But I had to go back in again. Sam, Adam, and Callie were watching cartoons while I heated leftovers.

I was waiting for Sandra to call too.

She was picking up the twins tomorrow.

I was nervous. I couldn't lie. It would be the first time she had them on her own over a whole weekend, without Kathryn nearby. Granted, Sandra knew she could call me whenever, and I actually believed she would. She didn't sit on any high horse. But one might say I was suffering from separation anxiety. Her connection with the twins didn't come naturally, something that continued to hurt. But she was trying, and we were holding out hope that it would get easier. The twins weren't babies anymore. They were three years old and had personalities and likes and dislikes. Adam was obsessed with Play-Doh, and Callie loved soccer and doing the hair on her dolls.

The latter wasn't fun for Jake and me. She could never get it right "like Auntie Nikki," which resulted in tantrums and chaos.

Either way, their ever-changing hobbies were something Sandra could use to get closer to them. One could hope.

"Roe!" I heard Jake call.

"Food's almost ready, kiddos. I'll be right back," I said.

Sam, Adam, and Callie paid me no mind.

I went back out front, only to come to a stop right in the doorway. Jake stood on the low stoop and filmed the boys. Colin was holding one of our hummingbird feeders, and Casper was the one talking.

"...and the sugar water helps the birds get more food, and that's good!" He looked up at Colin and whispered. "How much sugar was it?"

I smiled widely. They were too precious.

"One cup sugar and four cups water," Colin supplied.

"Yeah! So that's what we do." Casper beamed. "We have four feeders, cuz our dads say hummingbirds can fight and stuff if there's only one."

Fuck me, I was proud of them. Our little documentary-makers.

CHAPTER 2
2021

"What do you wanna do next weekend? We could go skydiving or hit up a nightclub?"

I barked out a laugh and threw a few boxes of frozen pizza into the cart. "So it begins. Jake Denver's midlife crisis."

All because he'd found a few gray hairs...

"Shut up," he grumbled.

He'd been in a bad mood because of this all week. When I told him I only found him hotter, which was the fucking truth, it seemed to go in one ear and out the other.

We kept filling our cart, and I did my best to distract him with work talk. After all, we had a lot happening. We'd recently come back from surviving a month in the Rockies. We were officially in preproduction on our Congo project. We had a new contract with Netflix. Award season was looking hella promising, and—

"Okay, we gotta get back to work." Jake was staring at his phone. "Seth texted. He found us a new headquarters."

Oh, fuck yeah. Jake and I were beyond ready to have the Condor Chicks house as just *our* office and podcast studio again.

We headed for the registers after I made sure we had the few items Haley had asked us to pick up. Seth's and her son was teething, so the little one was chewing on semi-frozen fruit all day long.

After loading up the car, Jake got behind the wheel. "Hey, I know what we should do. If not next weekend, then maybe the weekend after that."

"Yeah?" I buckled in and wondered if we should buy flowers or the most obnoxiously massive balloon for our new nephew.

"We should accept Greer's offer and put together a very late wedding shindig on his farm," he said, which definitely had my attention. "It's still warm in Virginia, the Brooklyn side of the family can swing short notice if they don't have to travel far, it'll be easier for Grandma to stay on the East Coast, and Andy is old enough to fly now."

I loved my gray-haired husband.

He had the best ideas sometimes.

I grabbed his hand and threaded our fingers together. "Best idea you've had today."

Bad enough we couldn't fit in our honeymoon until next year, literally two years after we got married. But with work, kids, more work, travel restrictions, safety measures...everything had been put on hold, and now shit was piling up.

CHAPTER 3

2022

I f someone told me...whatever, fifteen, twenty years ago, that one day, I was going to go on a honeymoon with my husband...and we would bring not only his ex but his ex's husband and... I wasn't even gonna finish that thought. To an outsider, it probably would've been weird. But here we were, in fucking Milan, with all our kids, Nikki, Russell, Haley, Seth, and their boy. And I wouldn't have it any other way.

At the rental place, it was time to do car math, because driving around Italy in a giant SUV just wasn't gonna happen. Or two, for that matter. No, this country was for tiny cars. Tiny cars for narrow streets and Italians who were...passionate drivers, even by my standards.

"Okay, listen up!" I held up the car keys. "Russell and Nikki, you take Sam and Callie in the green Fiat." I handed Russell the right key.

"Yay! We go together, Sammie!" Callie cheered.

The sisters were happy—and not just about going together; they were with Momma Nikki.

"Let's grab your luggage, ladies," Russell said. "We'll meet up at the hotel?"

"Perfect." Jake nodded.

I turned to Haley and Seth. "The red Fiat is yours, and you can—"

"Me, Daddy!" Adam said, raising his hand. "I wanna go with Andy."

Okay, fair enough. I was gonna suggest Colin because he was easy and little Andy was not, but maybe this was better.

I dipped down and kissed the top of Adam's head. "All right, then Daddy and I will grab the blue Fiat and toss Colin and Casper on the roof."

At least Cas found me hilarious. Colin, the preteen, graced us with a smirk.

Here we go. Honeymoon with the whole damn family.

Well, sort of. We all had different interests, and we couldn't bring the kids to every museum we wanted to go to because we'd get kicked out for some reason I didn't dare entertain. So for the first two days, we split up a lot. We took turns taking the kids to the sights they would love—more importantly, the activities they would love—while the second group got to gorge on history, ancient architecture, and endlessly long lunches at romantic restaurants. We had breakfast at the hotel together, and we met up for dinner before we bribed the kids to go to sleep because all the mommies and daddies were ready to pass out.

On the third day, *someone* had a bizarre idea. Fucking Jake, of all people, suggested we go shopping together. All of us. Shopping. With six kids. *Shopping.* In Milan.

Granted, the famous shopping street, Via Monte Napoleone, wasn't far from our hotel, so if Casper tore down a mannequin at Prada or Sam screamed at a Hermès salesperson, I could retreat quickly and seek shelter.

I'd do it too.

"Okay, everyone grab a kid," Nikki instructed.

I ended up holding Adam's hand firmly, and Jake swooped up Callie and placed her on his hip.

"You're all mine now, aintcha?" He pretended to nibble on her cheek.

"No, Daddy, stop it! I want a pretty purse."

Ah, happy fucking sigh. It would never get old hearing our kids cross over from one parent to another. Callie did it most frequently, with her twin brother a close second. Which made sense. As the youngest, they couldn't remember what'd come before our married bliss. Callie didn't mind calling Nikki her "Momma Nikki" either, hence our new nickname for her.

"You can have whatever the fuck you want, baby girl." Jake felt the same way I did. Also, he was whipped.

"You do know there are $30,000 purses in here, right?" I asked as a doorman let us in.

Jake cleared his throat, then whispered to Callie. "When we get to another store, you can have ten purses there."

I chuckled. "You've got yourself to blame. I'm still shell-shocked that this was your idea."

He sent me a sideways smirk. "You and I need finer threads for somethin' I've got planned."

Oh, *really...*

I lifted my brows.

"Daddy, look at the bling." Adam was mesmerized.

I decided to dig for answers later. I picked up Adam, and I was fairly sure one of the salesladies looked relieved.

There *was* an awful lot of bling in here. Gold and sparkles all over the place. Glass counters that didn't need smudgy fingerprints.

Colin and Casper had found seats, and they were busy playing on their phones. So no wonder Nikki and Russell were lookin' all flirty in the corner by the dresses. They weren't chaperoned by a kid.

"You wanna help Daddy find nice clothes?" I smooched Adam's cheek.

"That one!" He pointed at something with sequins.

My honeymoon continued. After Milan, we packed up the kids, countless souvenirs, and a fair number of shopping bags, and we drove our three tiny toy cars north toward Lake Como.

It wasn't a long drive, maybe an hour or so—traffic was a bitch—plus...the kids. Four stops to pee. Four. Then Nikki wanted a soda, Seth was hungry, and Sam had gotten gum in her hair.

It was wonderful.

Jake and I had the twins in our car, and we breathed a sigh of relief when they fell asleep. Around the same time, we reached the lake. Mountains everywhere. Little villages poked up from the green mountainsides, and my photographer of a husband hauled out his camera.

We stopped at every roadside parking spot along the way to the town of Bellagio. Long, narrow, winding roads framed the gorgeous lake, which was shaped like an upside-down-facing "Y." And Bellagio sat on the point in the very middle, where it overlooked the splitting of the lake.

13

The place was breathtakingly beautiful.

Maybe that wasn't a good thing? Jake was gonna wanna take a photo of every tree, every colorful house, the shutters, the flower beds, the whole nine yards.

I climbed out of the toy car and rubbed my neck. Our hotel was stunning too. Painted a rustic yellow with green shutters—and red roses hung from the balcony railings. Twenty-four hours. I had to get through the next twenty-four hours, and then Jake was promising an outing for just the two of us.

I didn't want more than that. Considering how much work we had, vacations were few and far between, especially to places like Europe. I was stoked everyone was here. But that didn't mean I wasn't going to appreciate the fuck out of a detour with my hubby. We needed some alone time.

This daddy hadn't gotten railed in a week. That was a record.

The day after, we all drove to a village that had a proper beach. It was small as hell, but we couldn't toss the little ones from a dock. They couldn't swim yet.

Jake excused himself to run an errand, and I kept my grin to myself.

What had he planned? Dinner somewhere, maybe? The villages around the lake were packed with romantic spots. Or perhaps a picnic along some hiking trail? He did love his scenic routes. And I never wasted a good hike. I wasn't twenty anymore. My abs required constant upkeep.

While Seth and Russell watched the kids play in the emerald-green water, I slumped down in a beach chair next to Nikki and rubbed sunscreen onto my chest. Haley had found a shaded patch of grass just next to the beach, where she was gonna take a nap with her boy.

It was hot today. Not a cloud in sight. Plenty of boats out on the water.

Colin and Casper jumped from an old dock, yelling "Geronimo!" and "Eureka!" each time.

"God, this is so nice." Nikki stretched out in her chair and adjusted her bikini. "You make sure to rest up before you're off to the freaking jungle."

I chuckled drowsily and glanced over at the kids. We were gonna miss them. Thank goodness for Skype, Zoom, and Face-Time. And Nikki, as always. She was gonna have the children more than usual since Sandra was off to her family place in France. She'd wanted to bring Casper along originally, and I was relieved as hell that he was the one who'd declined. He didn't wanna be away from his siblings and friends for that long.

Offering to bring the twins had been an afterthought, as if that would sweeten the deal and convince Cas.

It hadn't.

"How many film crews did you end up with?" Nikki asked.

I stifled a yawn and closed my eyes. "Six. Six crews, approximately two months on location for each." With Jake and me leading the main crew for the first and last month of shooting. But throughout the whole project, the crews would send us their footage for approval back in LA.

"Mommy! Daddy! Come, look!"

Me? I'm Daddy.

I cracked an eye open. It was Sam hollering, and since Jake wasn't here... She couldn't be referring to Russell. He was a wonderful stepdad to the whole bunch, but there was a fine yet distinct line that'd appeared pretty naturally; he was always Russell or Uncle Russell.

"What is it, sweetie?" Nikki called back.

I sat up straighter and squinted for the sun.

Sam came running for us with something in her hand. "I found a pretty rock! It's pink!"

She plopped down in my lap and showed us the flat pebble, and I tried not to wince at the cold. Fucking hell, either I had been in the sun too long—we'd been here less than an hour—or the lake wasn't warm enough to swim in. Christ.

"Very pretty," Nikki agreed.

"You should save that for your scrapbooking when we get home," I suggested.

Sam gasped. "I can put it in my album?"

"Of course," Nikki said. "We'll heat up the glue gun and go nuts."

"Yes, I want that. Can you keep it for me?" She extended the rock to Nikki, who tucked it into her purse.

Sam turned to me with a goofy smile, and she fell against my chest. "Hi. You're warm."

"You're not." I chuckled and wrapped my arms around her. "You wanna rest here with me for a bit?"

She nodded and laid her head on my shoulder, and she giggled softly. "Colin and Cas are clowns."

They totally were. Colin was doing flips right into the lake, and Cas was trying to mimic... He'd get there. Eventually. Maybe. He was a bit of a disaster.

Adam and Callie were more interested in sitting in the wash and playing with the sand.

It was a nice moment. I took some pictures and cuddled up with Sam, all while missing Jake. Was that ever gonna go away? Over the years, before and after we got together officially, people asked us if we ever wanted a break. Since we lived together, worked together, raised our family together. But no. Not once had I felt I needed a night on my own or something. Not from him. To me, the question alone was weird, because it was like asking, do you ever need a break from your lungs?

"Sweethearts!" Nikki hollered after a while. "Come get some snacks! It's time to reapply sunscreen too."

"Does that include me, love?" Russell smirked.

Nikki laughed and went all, "Oh, you."

By now, I'd covered Sam with a towel, and I wasn't sure she was awake.

I kissed the top of her head.

To think this slip of a girl was starting second grade soon?

"Can you hand me a water bottle, hon?" I asked.

Nikki glanced at me, then went back to handing out fruit and fun-sized bags of chips to the kids. "No, 'fraid not."

Excuse me?

She grinned and nodded at...the dock? "You're about to leave."

I was what?

I flattened my hand over my eyes to see clearer. All I spotted was a small boat approaching, and—wait. Was that Jake?

Nikki rose from her seat and carefully lifted Sam from my arms. She was definitely asleep.

I stood up, confused, and yeah, sure enough, it was Jake driving the boat. It was a smaller version of some of the speedboats docked in Marina del Rey, and it had a canopy roof—and two round windows below deck, indicating it had a cabin.

The romantic fucker had rented a boat for us.

"You knew all along?" I asked Nikki.

She snorted a laugh. "Of course I did. We all knew."

I wasn't gonna pretend to be annoyed.

Shit just got better from there. When Jake jumped onto the dock, I noticed he'd dressed up for the occasion. He'd put on his novelty Brooklyn Dodgers tee just for me. And the cargo shorts that made his ass look so fucking bitable. Last but not least, he'd dusted off the ratty USMC ball cap he'd often worn when we'd first met.

"He could've put on nicer clothes," Nikki muttered.

I shook my head and began walking down to the dock. No, this was perfect. This was my Jake.

He smiled at me as the boys crowded him, saying what a cool boat it was.

Colin wanted to drive it. Casper too.

"Over my dead body, boys," Jake laughed merrily. Then he picked up Casper and threw him into the lake to the sound of Cas guffawing. "Don't think I won't throw you in because you happen to be five feet, Bear." With a grunt, he hoisted Colin into the water too.

"Me now, Daddy!" Adam got all excited and held up his arms.

Jake chuckled, then exchanged a look with Russell out in the water, who approached. That settled it. "Okay, sugar. Remember to breathe out underwater."

Adam was tossed in close to where Russell stood, and all the boys were happy.

"Am I next, Daddy?" I joked.

He grinned and shook his head. With the last couple of feet separating us, he hauled me in close and gave me a smooch. "No, you're comin' with me. No need to grab anythin'. I have everything we need."

Well, hell. "You're gonna make me swoon, baby."

"I wanna say goodbye!" Callie yelled and ran for us. "See you in two sleeps!"

Whoa. I looked to Jake questioningly. We'd be gone for two nights?

He merely smiled and caught Callie between us.

"You be good and listen to the grown-ups, you hear?"

"I promise," Callie giggled.

"That didn't sound reassurin'." Jake chuckled and poked at her tummy. "But you know what? That's Momma Nikki's problem. Daddy and I are outta here."

We fucking were. Once we'd said goodbye to everyone, we jumped into the boat, and I was kinda blown away by the whole thing. The boat was sheer luxury in a tiny package. Up on deck, we had a fancy little seating area under the canopy, with a comfortable couch surrounding a table on three sides. Which Jake said could be turned into a sunbed if we flipped the table around.

Right now, said table had goodies for us. Strawberries, bread, grapes, a spread of cheeses and cold cuts, an open cooler on the floor with ice, wine, champagne, beer, soda, and water.

"Have a look below deck while I get us out on open water," Jake suggested.

"You're fucking amazing." I kissed his cheek and then squeezed my way down the narrow steps to the most luxurious little bunk. Perfect fit for us to get real intimate. We couldn't stand upright, obviously, so we'd be sitting on the comfy-looking bed if we were to get dressed. 'Cause I noticed the overnight bag, and we'd gone to all the trouble of buying fancy threads.

I just smiled and shook my head. What more could I need? There was even the world's smallest kitchenette, with a sink and a coffeemaker.

"Don't use the water, by the way," Jake called from the deck. "We'll need it for when we get ready for dinner."

Oh? Noted. Important to wash up and so on. Maybe I'd be thoroughly fucked by then.

I was ready to rock the boat.

We spent the next several hours just acting like newlyweds. Sometimes we anchored; sometimes we crawled along the shoreline and breathed in the scenery. The villages, the impressive mountains, the nearby boats.

We emptied the table and flipped it around, and we fanned out a few towels on the cushy leather sunbed. We made out lazily and drank champagne from the bottle. We were classy like that.

"This kind of reminds me of Norway," I murmured. "The nature, I mean." The mountains weren't as steep here, but it was a similar contrast. The high mountains meeting the water below, surrounding the lake completely like the deepest basin.

He hummed and dropped kisses along my abs. "We should go back there."

It was on the list. We wanted to bring the boys. They loved a good camping trip. The girls didn't.

I threaded my fingers into Jake's hair and scratched his scalp.

The sun was dipping lower, painting the bottom layer of the sky orange and pink. On one side, anyway. The other side whispered of a rainy night, and I didn't mind that at all. I could think of worse things than being stuck on a boat with my sexy husband while the rain pitter-pattered on the canopy ceiling.

"Come make out with me."

He kissed his way up my body, and we met in a languid, tongue-teasing kiss.

Just feeling his body pressed against mine was all the revving up I needed.

I slid my foot along the back of his calf and squeezed his ass to me.

"Mmm... We shouldn't take this too far," he murmured. Some bullshit, it sounded like. "We have dinner reservations in an hour."

"Oh." I lifted my head and glanced around us.

He followed suit and nodded at the shore. We were maybe a hundred feet out. "See the white house with green shutters?"

I saw it.

"Restaurant on the first floor, hotel on the second and third." He kissed me again, a slow, drawn-out one that made me forget where we were. "We're spending our first night there."

"You're just full of surprises." I deepened the kiss, excited about his plans but wondering if I could sway him on the not-taking-shit-too-far crap. We had an hour, right? I could do a lot with an hour.

"And you're makin' me hard, darlin'..."

I kissed him hungrily and slipped a hand between us so I could feel him through his boxer briefs.

Fuck me, I could never get enough.

He groaned under his breath.

"Would it be so bad to see how comfortable the bed is before we eat?" I asked. "It would be a shame to let it go to waste."

He inhaled deeply and pushed his cock against my hand. "We're sleeping there tomorrow, but you have a point..."

Score.

"We'll get ready for dinner soon." I nudged him back, and he just stared at me like he was ready to eat me alive. He'd get no complaints from me.

In a cabin that small, we had to get creative. Good thing I was bendy as fuck, and Jake had no problems nearly folding me in half.

He hooked an arm under my leg and drove in deeper, a bolt of fiery pleasure shooting through me with each thrust. My eyes widened before I screwed them shut and sucked in a sharp breath.

"Fuck!" I gasped. "Just like that. Oh God—oh fuck!"

He groaned against my neck. "I love when you lose your composure on my cock, baby."

I felt I did that very frequently. Since I couldn't move properly with him fucking me into the mattress, I had to resort to just swiveling my hips to meet his punishing thrusts. I cried out at the pain that sparked up, and I still wanted it again and again. At this rate, he was gonna get me off without me even touching my cock.

Holy fuck, I'd needed this today. Going a week without sex just wasn't like us.

"Keep goin'." He sucked on my neck and ground deeper. "I wanna hear every sound. This is what only I get to do to you."

I swallowed against the dryness in my throat, and a needy whimper slipped out. Years later, and he was still so possessive of me. Fuck, how I loved it.

"Only you." I grabbed his face and kissed him hard. "I love you so fucking much."

He shivered and pushed his tongue against mine so damn seductively that he made me shiver too. He slowed down, just for a second, long enough to whisper that he loved me too, that he loved I was his husband, before he started fucking me stupid again.

Supporting himself on the back of my leg that he kept his arm hooked under, he freed up his other hand and stroked me quickly. I almost fucking lost it right there. I cursed and moaned, gasped and pleaded—and drew out my dirty beast.

"There's my slut boy," he said, breathing heavily. "Don't come."

"Wh-what?" I choked out, eyes growing wide. "I'm too fucking close."

So he abruptly stopped touching me, and I cursed soundly. That fucker! Now wasn't the time for games!

Fuck, fuck, fuck.

The pressure had built up so much that I lost control of

myself. I just needed to get fucked. Fucked, fucked, fucked. By him. Hard, deep, mercilessly—till I came all over myself.

Jake laughed through a groan, and I could tell I'd lost him. He was already coming. He pumped his cock into me fast and shallowly, then slammed in deep and moaned.

I clenched down, craving the friction, wanting to milk the orgasm out of him, give him more pleasure, no matter how fucking frustrated I was. He knew it too. He felt me squirm and writhe underneath him.

Luckily for me, my man wasn't a sadist. The moment he came down from his high, he eased back and replaced his cock with three fingers. Filthy fuck—he loved sliding his fingers through his come in my ass.

"You're not making a mess of yourself when we have a dinner reservation." With that said, he sucked my cock into his mouth.

I moaned like the whore I was and arched my back. My fingers disappeared into his hair, and he sucked me off until I was coming down his throat.

My fucking God—and we had dinner now? Like, I would have to stand on my legs? Get dressed and shit?

"Jesus," I panted.

On the other hand, seeing Jake in his new clothes might spark a round two for later. It wasn't often we put on nice pants and tucked in our shirts. Or wore that kind of shirt at all. We were all about tees, jeans, cargo shorts, hoodies, and sweats.

Jake crawled up my body and kissed me passionately, and I couldn't help but moan at the taste of my come on his tongue.

"I'm gonna wash you up," he murmured. "Thoroughly."

I shivered.

"Before you mess me up all over again?"

"I promise."

I'd make sure he kept his word.

Half an hour later, we looked hella hot and walked hand in hand up the dock to the restaurant. Candles and string lights illuminated the little area, and this town was so small that I was surprised people knew it existed. An old church was next door too. And we were far from alone. Maybe some twenty people filled the restaurant, and we were the last to arrive for the eight-o'clock service.

We were shown to our table for two. We ordered first courses, second courses, wine, and desserts. I was...so fucking caught up in this romantic bubble Jake had planned for us that I barely noticed another dinner guest recognizing us. She asked for autographs before we were left alone again.

Jake grabbed my hand on the table, and I smiled.

He was just watching me, looking at ease and happy and in love.

CHAPTER 4
2023

"Thank you, guys. We'll be back in twenty minutes," I said, climbing out of the Jeep.

"No problem, take your time," Nswadi replied. "Henri and I wait here."

If my French could just be as good as his English, I'd feel a lot better. But I'd been studying an hour or so every night the past year, so I wasn't *bad*. I'd had a couple friends in LA, one who was French and one who was French Canadian, help me improve my vocabulary. And the grammar... Christ. However, Nswadi loved to practice his already good English around Jake and me.

Jake and I crossed the dirt road and ducked into the internet café. I wiped perspiration off my forehead and did my best to resist scratching all my two hundred mosquito bites. If they didn't kill me, the humidity might. The rainy season was about to begin, to boot. Everything was wet.

Other than that, it was hard not to love the DRC. The nature, the countless local cultures, the food, the *people*... Despite all the suffering, the corruption, the wars, we'd met some of the most hopeful and lovely men and women in this country. Going home wasn't going to be easy. At least last time, we'd been able to say *see you in a year*. Now, we were in the final stretch of our last month.

Claudia and Alphonse, who ran the café, knew us by now, and they were so interested in learning what we'd been up to since last time. We tried to come in every week for a Zoom call with the kids, but life in the rainforest didn't follow strict schedules.

Soon enough, we took our seats in front of one of the computers, and Jake logged us in. The walls were littered with flyers and posters about cheap international calls, travels, and sightseeing tours.

The internet connection was spotty this far outside the cities, but it didn't take too long before we saw...well, a few of the kids on the screen. I smiled and wasn't at all surprised to see Casper had a Band-Aid on his forehead. Adam and Sam appeared to be unharmed. It was early in LA, so the pajamas and bed heads made sense.

"What happened, son?" Jake chuckled.

"Hi!" Sam waved to us.

"Hi, Daddies!" Adam grinned, revealing a missing tooth. Too cute.

"Hey, sweethearts. How are you?" I asked.

"Good! I fell off my skateboard." Cas smiled sheepishly.

Jake and I weren't shocked. The boy was reckless.

I had no idea where he'd gotten that from.

Over the next ten minutes, they filled us in on how their past ten days had been, obviously all speaking at once, and we just soaked it up. Colin was "studying" for his and Casper's pitch to Jake and me. They wanted to do a second season of *Little Species*, only Colin wanted this one to be called *Endangered Species*—and Nikki was totally on board already, Cas informed us. Sam was rehearsing for a school play, and Jake and I assured her we wouldn't miss the opening night next month. Adam asked if he could skip next weekend with Sandra because he wanted to go to a water park with Auntie Haley and Uncle Seth. Jake and I told him to call Sandra first to make sure, though we didn't foresee any issues. It wasn't the first time Adam had canceled his time with Sandra; same went for Callie and even Casper. And who could blame them? Sandra's idea of fun was either to bring them along while she hung out with her girlfriends, or she left them with Kathryn. Sandra had met someone this year too, and the man lived in Chicago but was in LA on business a lot.

It was what it was, and so long as the kids didn't suffer, we let things be. The children were growing up, and custody was less about agreements and more about what the kids wanted for themselves.

Haley approached the computer in the background, and she asked for a moment with us.

"Okay, see you soon, love you, bye!" Casper ran off first.

"Bye, kiddo," I chuckled. "Love you all."

"Love you, knuckleheads." Jake smiled and squeezed my hand.

"See you next week, and happy birthday, Dads!" Sam waved. "We're gonna have a big party when you get home, right?"

"Of course, pool party and barbecue," I promised.

Jake wasn't particularly looking forward to his big fortieth in a few days, but it'd been much worse when he'd started finding gray hairs. I knew the feeling of that now too. And fuck it. We were still hot as fuck—maybe even hotter. According to some tweets and articles, we were sexy and charismatic.

Haley smiled tiredly and tucked a piece of hair behind her ear. "A couple things. Your fans are still rioting—half jokingly—about *Off Topic*."

Eh. They'd get over it. We weren't ending the show; we loved it very much. But every day was a lot, so we'd decided last year to drop down to a weekly episode. It was two hours long, had more exciting topics, and we invited guests more frequently. The number of viewers and listeners was still growing every now and then.

"You okay, sis?" Jake cocked his head.

Her smile faltered, and when her eyes welled up, I got worried.

"Um, yes and no." She sniffled and exhaled a soft laugh. "I wasn't sure whether to say this now or when you got home, but —anyway. I'm gonna change your flights home, because we have to go to Florida."

Oh no. She only had to say that much for me to get it.

Jake too. He sighed and scrubbed a hand over his face.

Fuck, fuck, fuck.

"Grandma passed away a couple days ago." She spelled it out. "I spoke to her nurse, and she died peacefully in her sleep."

"Goddammit." I swallowed hard and pressed a kiss to Jake's shoulder.

I mean, the lady had been ninety-six, so we'd kinda seen it coming.

It always sucked to lose a family member, though. Especially one who'd been such an important role model and support to Jake and Haley.

Jake cleared his throat and blinked back his emotions. "She wouldn't want a boring funeral. We'll celebrate her our way when we get to Florida."

Haley nodded and smiled, and she wiped her cheeks. "Apparently, she was prepared. She wrote a letter to the nurses a while back and got everything in order. Dad's not invited to the funeral. Or in Grandma's words, 'I will love my son until the end of time, but he's done lost his damn marbles. I will not have him at my funeral.'"

I spluttered a laugh and got all emotional anyway. What a Grandma Jo-Jo thing to say.

"Fuck—" Jake was on the same page. He chuckled and quickly wiped away a stray tear. "I'm gonna miss that woman."

Me too.

Unfortunately, we had to wrap up our conversation and get back on the road. Haley assured us she'd take care of our tickets, and she and Nikki would get started on funeral arrangements. Jake and I thanked her, and then the screen went dark.

We looked at each other.

Yeah, things were great and awful at the same time. It was a bizarre feeling, wasn't it? Josephine's time on this earth was really one to celebrate, and she'd lived a long and happy life.

"I think we need a detour." I touched his cheek and took the proverbial wheel for a bit. "We can be a few hours late." Our film crew wasn't going anywhere. They were back at our base-camp preparing dinner by now.

"What do you have in mind?"

A pick-me-up. He needed it. I could tell by the sorrow in his eyes.

An hour south of town, we were welcomed back to a very special place. Kevin greeted us with excitement and rambled about the progress since last time. Belinda had recovered from her parasite infection. Rosa wasn't limping anymore.

I shook Kevin's hand and smiled warmly, and I thanked him for letting us visit again. *"Merci beaucoup de nous avoir permis de revenir."*

The wildlife sanctuary he ran with a group of veterinarians and volunteers had become our break while in the Congo. If work got too exhausting, or if we missed the kids, we came here to get reenergized.

Jake had his favorite girl of the non-human variety here, and Kevin took us straight to the pen where Rosa was. It looked much like the little display park you'd see at a zoo, only this one was just an observation area. The mountain gorillas that the sanctuary rescued had a massive chunk of land in which they roamed freely during the day, part of their rehabilitation.

Most often, Kevin and his team rescued babies. Orphans who stayed in the same spot their mothers had been killed by poachers. The sanctuary raised them till they could return to the wild.

"Thank you for this." Jake kissed my cheek, then handed me his camera when he spotted little Rosa.

I didn't know her age, but she couldn't be old. She hadn't been here long. She ran up to Jake, her head reaching just above his knee, and she climbed up in his arms.

"Hi, precious girl." Jake smiled softly, and the two hugged as if they'd known each other forever. "Okay, I hope I don't butcher this. Roe's been tryna teach me French. *Tu es trop belle.*" He called her a beautiful girl.

I beamed and took photos. "You're too fucking cute. You said it fine, love."

Rosa wanted down again, and she grabbed Jake's hand and

tried to drag him along. I chuckled and waved him on. He needed the break. In the meantime, I took photos and talked to Kevin.

The little park directly attached to the mountain gorillas' section had plenty of playground contraptions and toys for Rosa to show Jake, and he was happy to tag along.

Places like this one were so vital. We'd obviously made a donation already, but I hoped we could help out more in the future. We wanted to come back and possibly bring the kids—if it was safe enough. We traveled with a security detail for a reason. Poachers were a constant threat in the rainforest, and they were well organized and carried military-grade weapons.

For a year now, we'd had crews follow a group of gorillas here in the Congo. Just for a few days at a time. We were covering more than one topic for our series, but the gorillas had definitely earned a special spot in our hearts.

If everything went according to our plans and hopes, we'd teach millions of people about the last remaining mountain gorillas when the series premiered worldwide. Thanks to the protection from sanctuaries and people who gave a fuck, the number of gorillas was rising, but that would stop the instant those organizations lost funding and support. It was a threat they lived with.

Kevin was looking forward to seeing the docuseries. He was all about raising awareness, and he was welcoming a new film crew in just a few weeks. They were gonna make a documentary specifically about the orphan gorillas here at the sanctuary.

Our Congo project had reminded me just why I'd become a documentary filmmaker.

Fuck.

I scratched my head and trailed toward Jake. He was squatting down on the ground while Rosa rolled around in the dirt like a goofball.

"Baby?" I came up behind him and scratched his neck lightly. "We gotta let the boys continue the *Species* series."

He squinted up at me, then looked back to Rosa. "It's possible I've been thinkin' the same. Maybe we should sit down with Ortiz. Go all in and...I don't know."

I nodded and took a breath. Yeah. It felt right. Turn it into a larger production. Leave YouTube behind and give the boys an honest chance—and be there for them properly.

CHAPTER 5
2024

"I'm so tired," Colin groaned. He turned his ball cap backward and threw away an empty water bottle in a nearby recycling bin. "I'm starting to understand why y'all come home so damn exhausted after a trip."

"Mission accomplished," Jake joked. He draped an arm around Colin's shoulders and steered him toward the lounge. "Just one location left."

Casper leaned against me, and I grabbed his bag and kissed the top of his head.

"You hungry, buddy?" I murmured.

He nodded and yawned. "Just—no chicken. No birds."

I chuckled and winced. The list of things he'd no longer eat was growing. But I admired him for it. He was so young, yet he'd already found passions and things he believed in. I'd had my own periods of activism in my day, and I still didn't eat farmed salmon. Marine life had always fascinated me—since the day I'd learned about the near extinction of sea otters.

When we got to the lounge, the boys trailed over to the buffet while Jake and I found a table.

We were tired too.

After spending a few months on the road, with breaks at home in between, we were nearing the end of their second season of *Species*. Their *Little Species* had done well on our YouTube during the pandemic, and now they had a whole network behind them for the highly anticipated *Endangered Species*. They were officially playing in the big leagues.

Jake and I were mildly terrified.

We'd covered the California condor for personal reasons. We'd spent two weeks in Bolivia filming the blue-throated macaw, one week in Florida to cover the American crocodile, three weeks back to Jake's favorite gorilla Rosa in the Congo, and two weeks in Norway for the blue whale. Now we were in New York in search of sane people.

I kid.

It was a layover on our way to Spain.

The upside was the timing. The boys were on their summer break, so we didn't have to worry about homework or homeschooling assignments. Not that they'd missed a lot. We had to remain firm on a few things, and school was one of them. We would allow them to pursue documentary film-making so long as their grades didn't tank and they slept all right.

When push came to shove, they were children, and we didn't want that time in their life rushed.

Jake nudged me and looked over at the buffet, so I followed

his gaze and spotted a woman our age talking to the boys. Something about her daughter—I couldn't decipher every word.

"What's she saying?" I asked quietly.

"Her daughter is a fan of *Little Species*," Jake murmured. "Now she's interested in studying butterflies. And she wants a picture..." He started to get up, but I put a hand on his leg.

I heard Casper.

"Only if you're comfortable," he told Colin. Then he turned to the woman again. "Also, like, please don't post the photo everywhere. Our dads don't like that."

I fucking melted. He hadn't turned *eleven* yet, and he was so mindful of Colin's more introverted personality.

They reminded me of two someones...

The woman turned apologetic, perhaps realizing her request was bordering on inappropriate, considering she clearly didn't see their parents nearby—and she assured the boys it was only for her daughter.

Colin seemed to relax, and the two posed for a picture, applying their best smirks.

I exhaled and turned to Jake. "I don't like this any more than you do, but I think we can trust the boys to handle this bit, at least."

He nodded with a dip of his chin. "Sometimes I forget Cas is just like you. You goof off and act like you don't know what you're doin', and then you step in and control any situation two certain Denvers aren't comfortable with."

I smiled and kissed his jaw. "We love our Denvers."

"And we'd be fuckin' lost without our Finlays," he chuckled quietly.

"You're stuck with us for life."

He returned my smile and ducked in for a quick kiss. "Can't wait to get stuck with you on vacation."

God, me either. We fucking needed this. It wouldn't be a

huge hoopla like our honeymoon, but once we'd spent ten days doing an episode on the endangered Iberian lynx, Nikki and Russell were flying over to Barcelona with the rest of the kids. We'd meet up with them there and drive north to the tiny town of Cadaqués for a couple weeks in the sun.

I'd seen pictures of the place, and I was really looking forward to it. The town was an old fishing village, nestled in the mountains. It was supposedly famous for having been the home of several painters and artists, which explained the high number of galleries drawing in tourists.

Art had never been my thing. I was just itching for time off in a beautiful location.

Cadaqués looked exactly like I'd seen in the photos. Primarily white houses graced the green hillsides, with winding cobblestone streets and countless little boats in the bay.

From the balcony of our adjoined suites, we saw the whole town, and nothing but a boardwalk separated us from the private beach below. It might actually be smaller than the one we'd visited at Lake Como.

Each morning, Jake and I took the boys out for a run. A tradition we'd started recently. Jake went one way with Casper, and I took another with Colin.

I hoped Adam would be interested in joining one day, when he was old enough, but so far, he showed zero interest in nature, hiking, wildlife, running—practically everything Jake and I enjoyed doing with the other two boys. Instead, Adam stuck to going bananas in swimming pools, and he was really into music too. To the point where Jake had dusted off his piano-playing skills and introduced Adam to a new world. Russell had been next. He played the piano too, as well as the harmonica and the guitar. Adam could sit next to him for hours and mimic the movements of Russell's fingers.

Safe to say, we knew what we were getting Adam for Christmas.

Colin and I jogged up another hill. The morning sun was starting to get hot. The town was waking up to a new day. We ran alongside the one-way path that followed the shoreline, and we were joined by cyclists and the occasional Vespa.

Places like this one made me think further into the future. I mean, one day, I wouldn't mind slowing things down. Maybe have a vacation home where Jake and I could take more time off and just be.

We'd been through so much and still had decades left to share.

Family members had gotten married, divorced, popped out kids, died, moved... My nephew Crew lived in LA now. Greer was happily married and had more kids than I could count. One of the perks of getting together with a man—or possibly more than one—who already had children. In no way was my brother monogamous. He lived on his farm with three other men, for chrissakes. Even Mira was married, and she'd once sworn to stay single forever. She'd probably never have kids, though. They just weren't her jam, outside of the Auntie role.

"Dad?"

"Yeah?" I swallowed dryly and tried not to pant like a madman.

"Are you doing Patagonia next year?"

"Oh—probably not." I heaved a breath and wondered if this hill would ever end. "Remember when we visited Uncle Greer and Uncle Archie last spring? Archie gave me an idea I kinda wanna sink my teeth into."

Greer's hubby had grown up partly in the UK, and we'd gotten to talking one evening about the food industry. How certain ingredients were labeled toxic and ended up being banned in Europe, while we inhaled them in the US. The investigative journalist in me needed something other than nature documentaries from time to time.

"Why?" I asked curiously.

He ran closer to me as a group of cyclists whooshed by, and he grinned sheepishly. "I was just thinkin'. When you and Dad go there, maybe Cas and I could join...?"

The boy had another idea, didn't he?

The trick with Colin was to wait him out. Coax him gently, then wait. It was how several of our morning runs had turned into long conversations on some roadside bench.

"You got a pitch for me or what?" I chuckled, out of breath.

Colin was barely winded. "Maybe. I mean...think about it. Third season, *Invasive Species*. It's possible I read about the North American beaver being one of those species in Patagonia."

Goddammit. It did sound like an awesome follow-up theme.

That made me curious, though. I'd *been* curious for a while —and when I asked Casper, his answers weren't as...well-thought-out, was the best way to put it.

"Is this a fun hobby for you, kiddo?" I wondered. "The film-making, the researching—or is it a dream for a future career?"

He didn't ponder for long. "I don't know yet. Like, I really love to learn stuff, and the episodes are kind of my test or presentation. You know?"

That made perfect sense.

"You have years to figure it out," I replied. "I'm just nosy." I winked.

He laughed. "Sometimes it's just about hanging out with Cas. It's probably weird my best friend is my dorky little brother, but he gets me."

I sighed happily, understanding exactly what he meant.

We spent the day on that slip of a beach in front of our hotel. We had everything we needed there. The boardwalk was littered with restaurants and cafés, so when we got hungry, when the kids wanted snacks and drinks, we didn't have to go far. The town managed to be both lively and sleepy all at once, boosting me with energy at the same time as the background noise never got to be too much.

Jake had brought our Bluetooth speaker and was torturing Nikki and me with country music. Jordan Davis, more accurately, because Adam *loved* him. Russell was Team Country, too, so Nikki and I had to save actual music for another time.

Russell sat on the other side of Nikki and hummed to the tune.

I picked up my plastic cup o' mojito and took a swig. The ice had almost melted in it.

"On three! One, two, three!" Colin, Sam, and Casper sprinted out into the water and dove under.

It got deep pretty fast, so we were glad all the kids could swim now.

"*Roe*," Nikki chastised under her breath. "You're moving to the music. Get ahold of yourself."

Shit. My bad. "I'll get better. I promise. Smack me if it happens again."

In my defense, country music was ridiculously dance-friendly. And I didn't know the Trouble Town Jordan Davis was singing about, but I had a husband who was welcome to go to Trouble Town on my ass. He was looking all delicious in his trunks. Perfect tan, fantastic body, killer smile. He tossed Callie over his shoulder and ran into the water to the sounds of her squealing.

I glanced over at Adam and smiled.

He'd brought his little guitar, and he was practicing for all he was worth. We'd stuck an umbrella into the sand by his towel because he tended to forget where he was.

"You're getting so fucking good, buddy," I said, incredibly proud of his dedication. Guitar, piano, bass, harmonica—he wanted to play it all, and he learned by tinkering along to country tunes. He didn't like sheet music.

He looked over at me and grinned. "Thanks, I almost know this song now."

"Don't forget to eat, rock star." Momma Nikki was always on snack patrol. She seemed to think the kids would starve or go down from dehydration if they didn't put something in their mouths every hour.

Adam dutifully tossed a strawberry into his mouth and chewed demonstratively for Nikki to see.

I chuckled.

"Much better." Nikki winked.

"Dad!" Casper yelled. "Don't be boring! Get in!"

What the fuck? *Boring*?

My son called me boring?

"Ohhh, he called you boring, Daddy," Adam laughed.

For the first and last time. Holy fuck. Nobody called me fucking boring. *Ever*. Goddamn kids these days. I rose from my towel, mildly annoyed, and brushed sand off my calves.

I scratched my jaw and eyed Adam. "You wanna show the punks how it's done?"

He nodded quickly and put down his guitar. "Hell yeah, are we gonna jump?"

Absolutely. Casper and Colin fucking booed as Adam and I took the steps up to the boardwalk—that didn't actually have any boards. It was a one-way, narrow street flanked by two stone sidewalks. Maybe beachfront was more accurate than boardwalk. Either way, the winding road went up a hill to the right, and Adam and I had jumped off the ledge a few times already. What it lacked in height—about three or four feet—we made up for in skills. 'Cause Adam had inherited his love of water from his old man, and he wasn't the only one who could do flips and shit.

Casper cracked up, swimming around in the water. "It's not even high! Anyone can jump from there."

"But can you do this, son?" I asked.

I exchanged a quick glance with Adam, and we nodded. Then we sprinted for the edge and did a flip into the water. Fuck me, my stomach flipped too. I was getting old! Shit like this never had fazed me in the past. Now I could barely go on a roller coaster ride without getting woozy.

I could fake it like a pro, though. Adam and I resurfaced to the sight of a scowling Casper. Jake and Colin were chuckling at him.

"It's so salty," Adam coughed. He cleared his throat and squinted.

I closed the distance between us and told him to blink hard. It would make the waterdrops near his eyes roll down his cheeks instead. The Med *was* a salty bitch, and it took some time to get used to.

"Better?" I touched his cheek.

He nodded and smiled like a dope. Then we swam over to the others so we could bask in Casper's huffiness. *Like, whatever, flips aren't that cool anyway.* He was cute. And I totally dunked him under the water for calling me boring.

Little shit.

CHAPTER 6
2025

"**G**oddamn, darlin'."

As long as that was his reaction, I wasn't gonna complain.

About getting fucking reading glasses.

I plopped down on my go-to sofa on the patio where I could oversee Adam and Callie in the pool. Jake could go back to manning the grill. I had more research to do, hence why we were spending the late afternoon at the Condor Chicks house. We'd banned work at home, but I had to get this done.

"I'll be your librarian tonight." I blew him a kiss.

"I'll hold you to it. Unless you mean an actual librarian

who's gonna recommend books on all the food I should throw out."

I laughed and opened my notebook. I guessed I'd gone all activist lately. But who could blame me? I'd been researching our food industry for about six months, and I'd only scratched the surface.

We'd made some...changes.

I used to find Jake's gardening endearing and even hot, 'cause he got all sweaty when he was at it. Nowadays, I encouraged it and didn't mind tagging along to buy seeds and whatnot. Because at the grocery store, I was seeing poison everywhere, so now I wanted us to grow more of our own vegetables and fruit. Jake had had to calm me down a couple times, which I appreciated. Shit was bad, but I couldn't let it take over my life. We'd made some compromises we were both happy with, eliminating the worst chemical sources and cutting down on a few others.

I wasn't the only one researching. Jake was going through reports and articles every night. We'd sit there in bed and just be horrified together. But he was better than I was at finding a balance.

Although, he'd actually proposed one change that was rather drastic. He was thinking about us possibly moving. And I wasn't opposed to the notion at all. We were kinda cramped here. The Condor Chicks house would obviously be ours till the day we died, but perhaps a house with a bigger backyard would be good for us. Jake wanted to get a dog now that the kids were older and could help out—and Ninja showed zero interest in learning tricks. I'd had to remind Jake a few times that Ninja was a *cat*.

We'd put Calabasas, Brentwood, and Sherman Oaks on the table as potential locations, 'cause we still wanted to stay in Los Angeles. Regardless, we weren't moving anytime soon; it would be when Adam and Callie were starting junior high or something like that. Maybe. But I did like the idea of living on the outskirts of a nice area not too far from here. Not smack-dab in the middle of wildfire territory, but not at the center of LA's perfectly square street grid either.

I tapped my pen against my chin and watched Jake flip the steaks we were having for dinner, and I could easily picture him with more open land in the background. Maybe a ranch? A nice one. With lemon trees and avocados and...a whole fucking orchard. A big barbecue area and pool for our rambunctious family get-togethers. And some peace and quiet when we wanted that too, which happened more and more lately.

Fucking hell, I was changing.

Where was the punk who wanted to go out every weekend?

I chewed on the inside of my cheek and peered down the aisle. Then up. It felt like the whole plane was asleep.

What was wrong with me?

Oh, I knew. It was that fucking house on Zillow.

Jake disappeared into the bathroom with our little toiletry kit to brush his teeth.

We didn't use to care about that shit for long-hauls and red-eyes. Brushing our teeth... Please, you did that when you arrived at your destination. But not anymore, apparently. I'd already brushed mine.

Callie and Sam were asleep in the seats in front of ours.

Goddammit. I got up and hurried over to the bathroom, and I knocked on the door.

"It's me," I said quietly.

Jake opened the door and looked utterly confused. "Somethin' wrong?"

Yeah. We were turning into old men who brushed our teeth

on red-eyes and didn't allow processed food in our house anymore.

Without explaining myself, I yanked Jake out of the bathroom just so I could enter first. And then I dragged him in again and reached behind him to close the door.

"Really?" He quirked a smirk, clearly still confused about my behavior—which was fucked up!—at the same time as it was pretty obvious what I was doing. I kissed him hard as I undid his belt and unzipped his jeans. But honestly, he was surprised. He *shouldn't* be. Right? Because I was Reckless Roe who had weird ideas.

Or I used to.

I sat down on the toilet and pulled out his cock, before I sucked him into my mouth.

He exhaled a chuckle and grabbed a fistful of my hair. "I'm gonna ask what sparked this—after I've come down your tight throat."

And I'd be honest with him, but I'd rather focus on his perfect cock right now. I closed my eyes and swirled my tongue around him, loving those moments before he got hard in a whole other way. He just felt so fucking good when he was still soft. Like a cuddle buddy for my tongue. I rubbed him against the roof of my mouth and braced myself for his desire.

A good blow job was a three-course meal. You loved the appetizer that woke up your senses and teased your hunger. Then soft went hard as a rock, and you got your entrée. You devoured it. You thirsted. You inhaled every bit of it. And we all knew what the dessert was...

"Fuck," he breathed. He rewarded me by loosening his grip on my hair and rubbing my scalp. "My sexy little cocksucker." And the dirty talk... *Hnngh.*

I sucked him through some turbulence like a good boy.

I hummed at the first taste of his pre-come.

He started fucking my mouth unhurriedly.

He wouldn't take long tonight. I knew his tells. He wanted to watch his cock slip between my lips for a minute or two, and then he'd pick up the pace till he came. And no matter why I'd ambushed him in the bathroom, he needed a release after the day we'd had. Back-to-back meetings, two interviews, an *Off Topic* episode, watching Casper's baseball game, dropping the boys off at Haley and Seth's, packing up the girls, heading to the airport...

I teased the tip of my tongue along the vein on the underside of Jake's cock and earned myself a groan.

His thrusts became sharper, and he sped up, pushing deep enough to rub the head of his cock against the back of my throat. My mouth watered, and I redoubled my efforts. Sucking him harder, running my blunt fingernails up and down his thighs, and peering up at him.

He loved that.

"Fuck, I love you. This beautiful face." He cupped my cheeks, then slipped his hands to the back of my head. "Swallow me down, baby. I'm gonna come."

A rush of lust tore through me, and then I got my dessert. He let his head fall back as he flooded my mouth with his come. I swallowed greedily and hollowed out my cheeks to milk the last out of him.

"Jesus fuck," he moaned.

Quiet, love.

When he was down to shivers and quick breaths, I sucked him clean and tucked him back into his boxer briefs.

He hauled me up for a hard kiss and cupped my face in his hands. "You gonna tell me what this was about now?"

I chuckled, a little out of breath, and zipped up his jeans.

He didn't smile, though. The affection was clear in his eyes, but so was the question. He wanted to know.

I looked down as I fastened his belt again.

Dammit. I was being an idiot. I guessed I was going through the same crisis he'd gone through when he'd found the first grays in his hair. Only for me, it was my behavior. My passions and my interests.

"I stumbled upon a house on Zillow, and all I could see were quiet nights on the front porch," I admitted. "Just you and me, looking out over the ocean."

His forehead creased. "And you don't want that."

"No, the problem is that I do." So I was just gonna be boring from now on, yeah? That was the deal? "That house—it's on the upper edge of Pacific Palisades, right near Temescal Canyon Park. We've hiked there. It's gorgeous and peaceful, and...I don't know. I used to wanna be in the middle of where everything happened."

Jake understood now. He touched my cheek. "How do you stumble upon a house on Zillow? There's literally no other reason to be on that site."

Well, whatever. Maybe I was looking at addresses. Maybe a listing on Zillow popped up in the search.

"This is actually your fault," I told him. "You put the idea of moving in my head."

He grinned. "I'm not sure you can put this on me. We were talking about a few years from now."

I huffed and opened our toiletry kit. "Don't act like you don't know me. We got what, two years till we reach preproduction on *Additives*? And I'm already researching every minute I can spare." I applied toothpaste to his toothbrush and handed it to him, and then I grabbed my own.

I was all for swallowing, but nobody liked come-breath.

"You're cute sometimes." He smirked and stuck the toothbrush into his mouth.

"Fuck you, I'm always cute." I started brushing my teeth

again, as one did on a red-eye when they were approaching forty hella quick. Two years to go. Go me.

"So tell me about the house, cutie pie."

I felt my mouth twitch. Bastard.

I kinda wanted to tell him about the house, though. It was fucking gorgeous. Hampton-style architecture that mixed old with new. From state-of-the-art appliances to exposed beam ceilings, from the new patio and pool deck in the back to the old oak trees in the front. Backyard view of the mountains, front yard view of the ocean. The property was significantly larger than what we had now, with its own grove filled with fruit trees and plenty of space for a dog to run around. Three bedrooms, though the home study could easily become a fourth. A fucking fireplace in the primary bedroom, a fully furnished guest studio above the garage...

Rather than rambling, I took out my phone and went to my bookmarks to show him the listing.

Yeah, I'd bookmarked it. Sue me.

Jake flipped through the photos while he brushed his teeth.

It was a house to grow old in.

I bent down as well as I could in the cramped space and spat out some toothpaste, then rinsed my mouth.

By the time I'd returned the toothbrush to the toiletry kit, Jake handed back my phone. He looked like he was concentrating, which meant he was thinking about logistics. He was turning and twisting the pros and cons, the potential problems.... He was undoubtedly thinking about the kids, just like I had already done.

Technically, nobody needed to switch schools until they were ready. We had the Condor Chicks house. We could list everyone there too. It was still a private residence; we just happened to work there. It actually looked more like a home these days too. 'Cause after Seth had moved our staff to Culver

City, the living room was once more a living room. The play-room for the kids had long since lost most of its toys. It was a guest room, a place for the children to do homework and watch TV.

"What did you think?" I asked carefully.

Jake snatched a paper towel and wiped his mouth. "That's our house. I'll call the agent when LA wakes up."

I lit up.

Holy shit, this might be happening?

"Don't look so surprised, darlin'." He grabbed my chin and planted a kiss on my lips. "The house is perfect. Whatever cracks and dents they're hiding in the photos, we can fix. We'll go to a showing, at least."

I hugged his bicep, too fucking excited. "I love you."

"I love you too." He smiled and opened the door, and we held hands like love-sick idiots on the way back to our seats.

London greeted us in the most London way.

It was pouring down.

After we got checked in at the Marriott next to King's Cross, we had some time left over to stuff our faces. So Jake and I brought the girls over to Nando's, 'cause it was real close, and Nando's was Nando's. We loved their chicken.

"We can sit over there!" Callie pointed at an empty table in the back. It seemed all of London wanted Nando's for lunch.

"You go sit down," I urged. "I'll order for us."

Jake nodded and ushered Callie toward the table.

"Dad, can you get the garlic bread?" Sam asked.

"Absolutely," I replied.

I ordered a *lot*. One whole grilled chicken for the table, comin' up. Extra wings, all the sides, sodas, let's fucking go. We were in London and had two daughters who wanted to shop. Granted, they were also here to visit Nikki, but the tourist magnet Harrods was tough to compete with.

We'd traveled so much with Colin and Casper for *Species* that it was time to even the score a bit. The girls had requested a city vacation "someplace cool," and Adam wanted to visit Nashville.

Jake could not be prouder of our boy. Adam was all country.

It was gonna be wonderful, though. Just us three for a few days. We'd take him to a couple shows and maybe buy him a new guitar.

Adam's music had sort of brought him and Callie closer too. They did have their special twin connection, but it hadn't been so tangible in the past. Now, though, we often found Callie sitting next to Adam when he practiced. She sang sometimes. Other times, she drew on her iPad.

It was nice to see, especially since Cas was so close to Colin. Adam was just a tad too young to have much in common with his brothers. On a day-to-day basis, anyway. The siblings were still close.

Casper's attachment to the twins came out in full force when he got protective; if he sensed Sandra wasn't being fair, which was most of the time, he got so mad.

Back in the day, Jake and I had made the mistake of worrying mostly about Adam and Callie, when we should have been more concerned about Casper. Because the twins were showered with attention by Nikki and Haley as well. In a way, the whole family had rallied around the twins to make sure they didn't feel left behind. But Casper was the one caught in the middle. Even more so now. He was old enough to understand, to see that something was fundamentally wrong with Sandra's lack of affection for Adam and Callie. And Cas was a Finlay. We were a loud, emotional, heated bunch. We got angry.

I'd been the same way growing up.

Before our food was ready, I fired off a text to him. He'd read it in a few hours.

Have a good day at school, buddy. Love you to pieces.

I could still get away with those messages most of the time. At twelve, he was right on that edge. The affectionate goofball and the cocky preteen. Jake and I could no longer hug him when we dropped him off at school, but we got them when he came home instead.

"Okay, remember what we said, girls. You stay close to us," Jake reminded.

"There's Sophie! And Mom!" Sam exclaimed.

"Sam." I raised a brow.

"I know, I know! I won't be in the way," she promised.

Callie grabbed my hand, more than a little starstruck to be on a movie set. She was watching all the people mill about on the otherwise empty street. I didn't wanna know what it cost to shut down a street in London. There was a reason a lot of movies taking place in this city were filmed in Wales.

Nikki was busy touching up Sophie's makeup, so we stayed in the background, on the sidewalk. It was kinda crazy. They had an assistant whose current job was to hold an umbrella over Sophie's head.

"We shoulda had that in the Congo," I said.

Jake let out a laugh.

"Back to your marks, everyone!" someone yelled. The AD, I bet.

Sophie slid off her chair and exchanged a few words with Nikki, before she glanced back to us with a smile and waved.

"Oh my gosh, be cool." Sam waved back.

I chuckled under my breath.

"Quiet on the set! Cameras rolling!"

Nikki beamed and hurried over to us. "My beautiful girls, I've missed you so damn much." She gathered them in a tight hug.

I slipped my hand into Jake's.

We knew the feeling. Nikki might have it worse, though. She'd been over here six weeks and had three more to go. At least she had Russell here. Those two were almost as inseparable as Jake and me.

"Let's go over to craft services," Nikki suggested, keeping her voice down. "I wanna know everything. Then you're all mine tonight. We're gonna kick Russell out and have a movie night with pizza and cake."

That sounded right up their alley. Jake and I were looking forward to a guys' night in a pub with Russell and Sophie's husband.

CHAPTER 7
2026

"Sweetheart, could you run down and grab a couple lemons in the grove and give them to Uncle Archie in the kitchen?"

"I s'pose! I'll be right back." Callie grinned and darted outside.

The dogs ran after her.

I followed her out too but stayed on the patio and set the wineglasses on the table. "Adam, Sam, Colin! Time to get up!"

They'd been in the pool all day, it felt like. Talk about a record-hot winter. It'd been over eighty-five all of October, and halfway through November, we were still in the low eighties.

"What time is it?" Colin hollered.

I checked my watch. "Almost seven."

"Shit." Yeah, that lit a fire under his ass. "Callie!" he yelled across the backyard. "Are you comin' with us to Ma?"

"Yeah!" she answered.

I walked over to the grill where Greer had been left to his own devices, and I handed him a new beer and opened my own too.

"It's never a good thing when you're quiet, big brother."

He chuckled and gestured vaguely around us with the tongs. "I'm just processin', kid. This place... It was a good move."

Yeah, we were happy. It was a beautiful house. We had so much more space.

We'd had a lot of greenery in MDR too, but everything was bigger up here. The old oak trees, the gardens, the pools, the patios, the hedges.

"And how fuckin' tall did Colin get since last time?" Greer shook his head and flipped the chicken breasts on the grill. "When you told me you got him a car for his birthday, it didn't compute in my head. He's supposed to be twelve."

He was supposed to be *five*.

Instead...he was sixteen and officially my height.

He'd probably get a couple inches taller too.

"Now you know how Jake and I felt when youse told us Jason got in to NYU," I laughed.

Between Greer, Archie, Sloan, and Corey, they had six kids spanning the ages of eighteen and five. They all lived together, though to save the youngest kids from confusion, they weren't an official foursome. It was Greer and his hubby Archie, then Sloan and Corey, who were also married.

"Don't get me started on that one," Greer said. "He wants to become some sort of technical engineer. I don't understand half of what he's talking about."

Jesus. I wouldn't either.

I took a swig of my beer and watched Colin usher the other kids inside. They had to step on it if they were gonna make it to Nikki and Russell's. Only Casper and Adam were staying here tonight, and Cas hadn't ventured downstairs yet. I was giving him time.

"My gosh, I'm hurrying," Callie said. "I'm just gonna give the lemons to Uncle Archie. You can go shower. You stink chlorine, stink boy."

"I'll throw you in the trunk," Colin replied.

"I'll mess you up!" Callie yelled.

I grinned to myself. The attitude on that girl sometimes. She reminded me a whole lot of my sister.

"Oh great, another Mira in the family," Greer mused.

"Right?" I laughed.

Someone put on music in the living room, and since it was country music, I could only guess it was Adam.

I sighed contentedly and turned around to just...soak everything in. The house, the trees, the seating area. The potted plants on the floorboards that Jake and Callie took care of together. Lots of herbs.

I glanced up at the window of Colin and Casper's room, and my heart squeezed uncomfortably. I'd give him another twenty minutes. I wanted him down here for dinner. Seeing family would hopefully cheer him up.

We had a surprise for him and Colin too. We were gonna let them move in to the guest studio above the garage. They'd wanted it since day one, and Jake and I were the parents who were trying to cling to the days our sons didn't want so much privacy. But it was time. We knew that. They maintained good grades, they were helpful around the house, and their teenage rebellion had so far been incredibly mild.

"I talked to Cullen yesterday, by the way," Greer mentioned.

"Yeah?"

He nodded with a dip of his chin and looked up at the house too. Then back at me. "I don't think you've heard this enough, but Aunt Nilla and Uncle Roy woulda been incredibly proud'a you, Roe."

Well, fuck. That one smacked me right in the gut.

"Thank you." I swallowed and averted my gaze back to the house. Ironic, wasn't it? I was a year away from turning forty, but being around my brothers sometimes made me feel like a twenty-year-old again. "I hear them sometimes in my head. Or I imagine what they'd say around the kids when they're up to no good."

"Uncle Roy would've taken bets and spurred them on."

I exhaled a laugh and felt a little emotional. Yeah, that was my dad. He'd riled up Francis and me sometimes back in the day.

"Has anyone seen Sloan?" Corey came out on the patio, looking a little panicked.

"He and Jake ran out to buy more beer," Greer answered. "What's wrong, boy?"

Corey was...around thirty, I was fairly sure, but he looked younger and carried himself in a certain way. When he was worried or anxious about something, it showed.

"I need help," he said. "I don't know how to turn my Insta private."

Greer furrowed his brow.

Corey smiled sheepishly and rubbed the back of his neck. "Yeah, so I took a selfie in front of Roe and Jake's award cabinet, and I tagged them in the photo, and now I have a bunch of their followers commenting."

I burst out a laugh and walked over to him. "I'll help you."

Christ, this guy was funny.

"Daddy!" Dylan, their youngest, ran out too. He was the only one they'd brought out to LA this time. The others were spread out between grandparents and college. "Can we go in the pool now?"

Greer extended a hand. "After dinner, buddy. Come here, you can help me put the burgers on the grill."

I knocked on Colin and Casper's door.

"Can I come in, sweetheart?"

Colin had just left with Sam and Callie, so Cas should be alone in there.

"I guess," was his muffled reply.

I opened the door and poked my head in, finding him in bed on his side of the room. He was just staring up at the ceiling.

This couldn't go on any longer.

I stepped inside and sat down on the edge of his bed, and I gave his leg a squeeze. "Talk to me, Cas."

He sighed and clenched his jaw. "I can't stop being angry, okay?"

"At Mom," I assumed.

Ninja crept out from under the bed and stretched on the rug.

"Well, yeah." Cas sat up and hugged his knees loosely. "I don't wanna fucking go to her place anymore."

I winced. *Language.*

Not the time to remind him.

"You don't have to. We've told you that," I replied gently. "I've said this before, and I'll say it again. You have to do what you feel is best for you, Casper. Whatever makes *you* happy— because you're the kid here. You have zero obligation to feel responsible or—I mean, I know you, son. You feel guilty, right?"

He dropped his gaze and nodded slightly.

My fucking heart. I scooted closer and cupped his cheek. "Listen to me. You've done nothing wrong. You're protective of your brother and sister—and I love you even more for it. But you're way too young to shoulder the role of a protector. That's my job. And if you're not comfortable spending more time with Sandra, I will handle that with her."

He blew out a breath and scrubbed his hands over his face. "I just wish she could give a shit about them too."

Yeah, me too.

We were so fucking relieved that Adam and Callie didn't appear to suffer much. They were just now reaching that age where they started having questions, but when push came to shove, they'd never had a bond with their mother. When Jake and I told the kids it was time to pack up to go to Mom, they automatically assumed it was Nikki. She was the one who welcomed them into her arms every damn time she saw them. The occasional weekend they went to Sandra, it was a chore. They brought their phones, iPads, and power banks to make sure they had something to do, 'cause she didn't engage. She barely did that with Casper either, though their relationship had still been different until recently.

She had at least asked him what he wanted to do.

Kathryn remained the godsend of that family. At Gramma and Grampa's house, Casper and the twins were treated equally —*spoiled* equally—and Cas could relax there, knowing that no one was playing favorites.

"You know you don't have to make any permanent decisions, right?" I reminded him. "It's totally okay if I just let Sandra know you want a break. Relationships change and evolve over time—it's possible you will find your way back to—"

"It's not about me, Dad," he said and looked up at me. "Do you think her relationship with Adam and Callie will change? Honestly."

I suppressed a sigh, and my shoulders slumped.

"Exactly," he finished.

I was so torn. If I were Cas, I'd say the exact same thing he was saying now. I'd feel just like he did. But as his father, I felt the need to remind him he could think more about himself, because that was true as well.

I heard a knock on the doorframe, so I turned my head and spotted Jake there.

"Did you tell him, son?" he asked.

I frowned, confused.

Casper nodded.

Okay?

Cas flicked me a glance. "I already told him I didn't wanna go back to her place."

Oh.

"It's nothin' against you," he added. "He's just not as diplomatatic as you are, cuz you feel like you gotta keep the peace."

I smiled at his pronunciation, unable to help it. I loved those moments when he wasn't so grown up after all. "First and foremost, I'm on your side. On Adam's and Callie's side. But you're right, I wanna avoid unnecessary fights." I gave his knee a gentle squeeze. "That doesn't mean I *won't* fight, though. Okay? I'll take a fight with Sandra any day of the week if it protects you from feeling bad."

Jake came closer and squatted down in front of the bed. "And you remember what I told you about the peacekeepin'?"

Casper nodded. "That Dad doesn't always mean what he says. Like, sometimes he wants to say stuff that isn't appropriate."

I pinched my lips together, part confused, part amused, 'cause I had a feeling Jake had been blunt with Casper.

"Correct," Jake replied. "You're old enough to know that Dad and I have to hold back every now and then, but we get pissed off too." He made eye contact with me, a sober expression on his face. "I don't want him to feel alone in his anger."

I drew a breath and nodded automatically. Those last words connected the dots for me, and he was so right. Fuck, the last thing I wanted was for Casper to doubt whether his anger was justified. Or like Jake had said, that our boy felt alone with those feelings.

"Cas, if I had a nickel for every time I wanted to scream at Sandra, we'd still live here, because this house was ridiculously expensive," I told him. Using a pinch of humor always worked to steal some of the tension in his shoulders. "You have every right to be angry, buddy. And I'm sorry if I've made you feel like you couldn't express that."

He shook his head. "You haven't, but it's nice picturing you angry with her. It may sound weird, but it's comforting."

It wasn't weird at all. If we felt someone was being mistreated, we didn't wanna be alone in the outrage.

"Nothing weird about it," I promised. "I guess I've been so focused on not wanting to be that parent who badmouths the other parent."

"That's what you said too," Cas told Jake.

Jake was rubbing Ninja's belly. "Yup. That's our Roe. And you know—" He faced Cas again. "It's me too. But we're not badmouthing Sandra. We're putting our foot down because we don't think she's bein' fair. There's a difference."

He was right again.

I rubbed Cas's knee and got his attention. "I'll call her on Monday, and I'll tell her whatever you want me to tell her. I can say you don't feel comfortable when Adam and Callie don't receive the same amount of attention, or I can let her know I'm the one noticing the special treatment and that I won't stand for it anymore."

He bit his lip and thought about it for a second. "I think I want her to know that I'm not comfortable. I mean, you've told her before, right? I remember when I was little and she wouldn't hold them. You whisper-shouted at her."

I winced. Some of those memories were worse than our thirteen-year-old son using the f-word.

"You can think about it this weekend," Jake proposed. "But right this second, I really wanna shoo y'all down the stairs, 'cause we have steaks waitin' on the patio, and Uncle Archie made his double-fried fries."

I smiled and raised a brow at Cas.

He couldn't fight his grin, or his relief, and that last one mattered the most to me. "Yeah, okay. I guess I could eat."

Now we're talking.

I hauled the boy off the bed and ushered him out, all while hugging him from behind and smooching the side of his head. "We love you, buddy."

"Yeah, yeah, love you too and all that crap," he snickered.

Jake chuckled. "I'll take it. It's more than what Colin gives us."

Aw, Colin had his moments too. Never in public anymore; he couldn't possibly be affectionate with us when others might see. But whenever he was tired, or when he was having a shitty day, he wanted to sit close to us on the couch. Sometimes even rest his head on our shoulders.

Casper was back to his boisterous self the moment we stepped out on the patio, and he was greeted by one loud faction of our East Coast family.

"Hi, Cas!" Dylan waved excitedly.

"Look who it is!" Greer exclaimed. "Will you fuckin' stop growin', boy?"

"Will you fuckin' stop askin', Uncle Greer?" Cas mimicked. "I'mma be taller than you! Hey, Dylan. Hey, all the uncles."

"Let's eat!" Jake said, rubbing his hands together.

"Sit here, Dad!" Adam patted the spot next to him. "We already started. Warning—there's lemon in the salad."

I chuckled.

CHAPTER 8

2027

"Good morning! You're Off Topic with Roe Finlay and Jake Denver. I'm Roe, and Jake's like a pig in shit today because he's no longer the only one on the wrong side of forty in our marriage."

Jake grinned into his coffee mug. "That's right, it's Roe's birthday, and we're celebrating it by flying halfway across the world."

"The things we do for work," I chuckled. "Jake and I are officially in the production stage of our most secretive project yet. It's gonna be another couple years before you see what it's about, so we won't frustrate you with vague bullshit. We'll just say, it's gonna be interesting visiting Belgium for interviews with some higher-ups in the EU."

"Because I hear politicians are always trustworthy," Jake said.

I laughed.

"We have some other news too," he chuckled and moved us along. "Every now and then, we gotta take a moment and just say we're so fucking proud of our eldest boys. Colin and Casper are currently outside the studio medicating their nervousness with pizza and Red Bulls because the third season of their *Species* series premieres tonight."

"Oh yeah, you don't wanna miss it," I said. "The third season is all about invasive species, which will cover everything from the Burmese python in Florida to feral peacocks—two of which actually live on our street. *Man*, do they get loud during the mating season."

"I may have considered getting a shotgun," Jake joked. Only, it wasn't a joke.

I smirked and checked my tabs on the laptop.

"I'm not gonna reassure everyone by saying he's kidding," I said. "Moving on! Can we talk about birthday cakes and how the ice cream variety should be outlawed?"

"If that's a hint, you should know me better. I'm picking up your favorite before lunch."

I grinned. I hadn't actually been worried, but I was passionate about birthday cake. "Hey, I'm just a forty-year-old dude who wants to talk cake."

He snorted a laugh.

CHAPTER 9
2028

"**C**an y'all calm the fuck down?" Jake arrived at our picnic table at the same time as I did. "You were quieter when you were babies!"

The kids piped down.

I kept my laughter at bay and unloaded all the dishes I'd brought over. "Tempura chicken sliders for Sam, tacos for Colin, burnt ends with fries for Adam and Callie, and sodas for everyone."

Jake was next. "Family platter of barbecue for Cas, carnitas for Roe, lobster roll for me, extra wings and fries for the table, banana split and mini donuts for dessert—I think that's it! I'm gonna dig in. If you want somethin' else, get it yourselves."

I sat down next to him and gave his cheek a smooch. Poor baby, he was too hungry to stand in line again.

"Hey, we offered, Dad," Colin pointed out.

"Don't mind him," I chuckled. "He's just jet-lagged. Give him a Snickers, and he'll be fine."

"I swear," he grumbled at me. But he couldn't hide the mirth in his eyes.

Yeah, we were exhausted, but it'd been ages since we'd had everyone together for a food-truck Thursday. Jake and I always went if we were in town, but to get the kids to join us...? Fuck me. Adam and Callie were still young enough. They went with us. But between Sam's soccer practice, Casper's baseball, and Colin surviving his first semester at UCLA, our family was pretty fucking scattered.

"I could totally go for a deep-fried Snickers," Callie informed us.

"Aw, *man*," Cas complained. "Now I want that too!"

"Boy, you're eating for a whole family already," I laughed. He was in the middle of some phase where he was eating at all hours of the day.

He smirked and patted his stomach. "There's always room for more."

Christ, it was like looking in a mirror...if that mirror shaved twenty-five years off my life.

"As long as you keep that T-shirt on," I replied and dug into my carnitas.

Jake snorted around his lobster roll. Yeah, we found it funny how every goddamn picture Cas posted online had to showcase his abs.

"Don't be jealous, Dad. It's not a good look on you," Cas said.

Jealous? Fuck that. I was fit. For my age. My abs showed when I tensed up really hard. Really, really hard.

"I can still outrun you, so shut up," I answered.

Jake shook his head in amusement. "Don't worry, son. Roe didn't mind flashing his abs online when we were training for Alaska. The apple doesn't fall far."

"It was one photo!" I exclaimed. "Haley posted it as a *joke*."

"They're a joke now too," Cas goaded.

I raised my brows at him. That little shit. "You and me tomorrow—we'll see who can lift the most at the gym."

"Bring it!" He widened his arms. He'd look cool if his face weren't smothered in barbecue glaze.

I loved my husband a little bit more for capturing it on his phone.

"Don't post that anywhere!" Cas yelled. "I have a reputation, you know!"

Colin coughed around his tacos.

"Send it to me, Daddy!" Callie got excited. "I'll post it *everywhere*."

"Why are you all so loud?!" Adam shouted. "I'm trying to eat here!"

"Honestly. People are staring," Sam said.

Jake and I glanced at each other.

This was what we'd asked for, right?

Yes. Yes, it was.

CHAPTER 10
2029

"We're in agreement when I say this is fuckin' nuts, right?"

"Oh yeah." My smile had never felt equal parts fake and genuine like this before. 'Cause I was so nervous I wanted to throw up, at the same time as, yeah, finally, we were fucking *here*.

The camera flashes were blinding.

The carpet was hella red.

People were louder than the Finlays.

Jake and I were suited up like penguins.

Welcome to the Oscars.

We smiled for the cameras and moved along as assistants with headsets directed.

My grip on Jake's hand hadn't been this tight since we'd been evacuated in a helicopter off the shore of San Diego more than ten years ago.

He squeezed my hand and leaned close. "Whatever happens, darlin'..."

Yeah. I nodded once. We'd covered this.

"I know, baby."

We were happy to just be nominated and such crap.

I took a steadying breath, and we were ushered to a reporter who stuck a microphone in our faces.

"Jake and Roe! Can you believe this? You must be so excited —and you look amazing tonight. *The United States of Additives* is nominated for Best Documentary Feature Film. How nervous are you on a scale of chill *Off Topic* episode to holy smokes, we're filming in the Andes?"

Jake exhaled a laugh while I grinned and shook my head.

What the fuck could we say?

EPILOGUE
2030

The first time we'd visited Big Sur, he hadn't had those laugh lines or the silver at his temples. His smirks and grins were tinted with discomfort and nerves back then too.

We'd been so wide-eyed and new.

Eventually, we'd come back to this place again. We'd hiked with the kids here. We'd gotten married here...

I leaned back against the edge of the picnic table and just watched Jake take a few photos of the view. Of the cliffs, of the sea.

They'd replaced the picnic table since we'd been here last

time. It was in better condition but filled with burn marks and graffiti.

I took a deep breath and reveled in the silence. Not even a breeze to stir up a rustle in the trees behind us.

The sun was about to set.

Twenty years.

I folded my arms over my chest and thought about everything we'd been through—everything that had changed. And the things that hadn't. At home or out in the field, I would never find my husband without a ball cap on backward. I was never gonna learn how to cook pasta, despite Archie's fervent attempts.

Jake came back to me and stowed away his camera. Then he half sat against the edge of the table, too, and draped an arm around my shoulders.

Tomorrow was gonna be busy. Adam and Callie had a recital. Colin was coming home from college for the weekend. Sam was getting her first car... Cas had a job interview with Ortiz.

Jake nudged me a little and nodded toward the sky.

I followed his gaze.

How fucking perfect. Two condors gliding through the sunset.

I tilted my head and smiled, and he smiled back and rested his forehead to mine.

Bring on the next twenty years, baby.

ABOUT Cara

I'm often awkwardly silent or, if the topic interests me, a chronic rambler. In other words, I can discuss writing forever and ever. Fiction, in particular. The love story—while a huge draw and constantly present—is secondary for me, because there's so much more to writing romance fiction than just making two (or more) people fall in love and have hot sex.

There's a world to build, characters to develop, interests to create, and a topic or two to research thoroughly.

Every book is a challenge for me, an opportunity to learn something new, and a puzzle to piece together. I want my characters to come to life, and the only way I know to do that is to give them substance—passions, history, goals, quirks, and strong opinions—and to let them evolve.

I want my men and women to be relatable. That means allowing room for everyday problems and, for lack of a better word, flaws. My characters will never be perfect.

Wait...this was supposed to be about me, not my writing.

I'm a writey person who loves to write. Always wanderlusting, twitterpating, kinking, cooking, baking, and geeking. There's time for hockey and family, too. But mostly, I just love to write.

~Cara.

Get social with Cara
www.caradeewrites.com
www.camassiacove.com
Facebook: @caradeewrites
Twitter: @caradeewrites
Instagram: @caradeewrites

Printed in Great Britain
by Amazon

23465266R00046